JULIÁN AT THE WEDDING

To Danny

Library of Congress Catalog Card Number pending. ISBN 978-1-5362-1238-9.
This book was typeset in Godlike. The illustrations were done in watercolor,
gouache, and ink. Candlewick Press, 99 Dover Street, Somerville,
Massachusetts 02144. www.candlewick.com.
Printed in Shenzhen, Guangdong, China.
20 21 22 23 24 25 CCP 10 9 8 7 6 5 4 3 2 1

Jessica Love

CANDLEWICK PRESS

This is Julián.

And this is Marisol.

Today they are going to be in a wedding.

Those are the brides, and that's their dog, Gloria.

A wedding is a party for love.

"Let's go," whispers Marisol.

"It's a fairy house," whispers Julián.

"Marisol?"

"Oh."

"Uh-oh!"

Julián has an idea . . .

"I got dirty."

"Yes, mija, but now you have wings!"

"There you are!"

And then there was dancing.